EXPLORING COUNTRIES

Panama

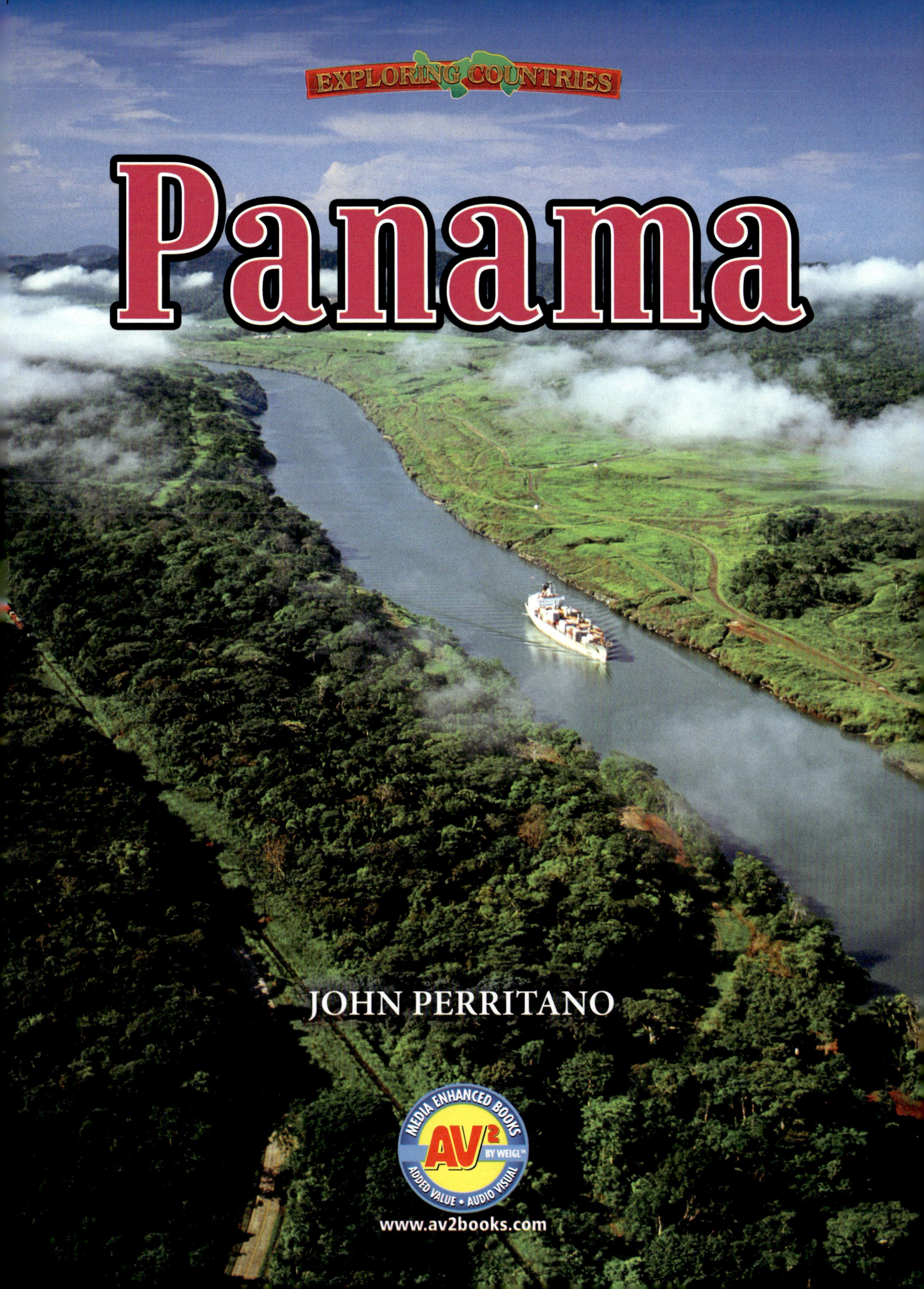

JOHN PERRITANO

www.av2books.com

Go to www.av2books.com, and enter this book's unique code.

BOOK CODE

AVQ74548

AV² by Weigl brings you media enhanced books that support active learning.

AV² provides enriched content that supplements and complements this book. Weigl's AV² books strive to create inspired learning and engage young minds in a total learning experience.

Your AV² Media Enhanced books come alive with...

Audio
Listen to sections of the book read aloud.

Key Words
Study vocabulary, and complete a matching word activity.

Video
Watch informative video clips.

Quizzes
Test your knowledge.

Embedded Weblinks
Gain additional information for research.

Slide Show
View images and captions, and prepare a presentation.

Try This!
Complete activities and hands-on experiments.

... and much, much more!

Published by AV² by Weigl
350 5th Avenue, 59th Floor
New York, NY 10118
Website: www.av2books.com

Library of Congress Cataloging-in-Publication Data

Names: Perritano, John, author.
Title: Panama / John Perritano.
Description: New York, NY : AV2 by Weigl, 2018. | Series: Exploring countries | Includes index. | Audience: Grade 4 to 6.
Identifiers: LCCN 2017055787 (print) | LCCN 2017056951 (ebook) | ISBN 9781489675156 (Multi User ebook) | ISBN 9781489675149 (hardcover : alk. paper) | ISBN 9781489680822 (softcover : alk. paper)
Subjects: LCSH: Panama--Juvenile literature.
Classification: LCC F1563.2 (ebook) | LCC F1563.2 .P47 2018 (print) | DDC 972.87--dc23
LC record available at https://lccn.loc.gov/2017055787

Printed in the United States of America in Brainerd, Minnesota
1 2 3 4 5 6 7 8 9 22 21 20 19 18

032018
120817

Project Coordinator Heather Kissock
Art Director Terry Paulhus

Photo Credits
Every reasonable effort has been made to trace ownership and to obtain permission to reprint copyright material. The publishers would be pleased to have any errors or omissions brought to their attention so that they may be corrected in subsequent printings.

Weigl acknowledges Getty Images, Shutterstock, and Alamy as its primary photo suppliers for this title.

Contents

Panama Overview

The small country of Panama, located in **Central America**, links North and South America. Each year, thousands of ships pass between the Atlantic and Pacific Oceans through a human-created waterway called the Panama Canal. Before the canal across Panama was completed in 1914, these ships had to travel all the way around South America. Panama's **economy** depends on the canal. Most Panamanians are of Spanish descent. Panama, which was a Spanish **colony** and then part of Colombia, became independent in 1903. Most residents of Panama are located in and around Panama City. Indigenous People live in the country's forests. Panama's beautiful islands, rich culture, varied plant and animal life, and historic canal attract visitors from around the world.

The Bridge of the Americas spans the Pacific Ocean entrance to the Panama Canal.

Fresh seafood, sold in street markets, is a food staple in Panama.

A variety of colorful flowers, including hibiscus, grow in Panama's warm climate.

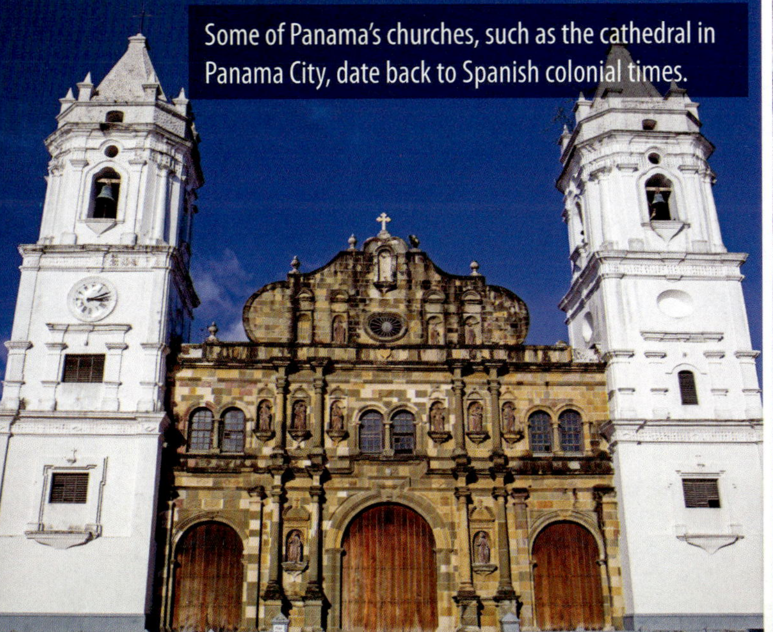
Some of Panama's churches, such as the cathedral in Panama City, date back to Spanish colonial times.

Parades and festivals are held throughout the year to celebrate Panama's various cultural groups.

Exploring *Panama*

Panama covers a total area of 29,120 square miles (75,420 square kilometers). The country is an isthmus, a narrow strip of land with water on both sides that links two larger areas of land. To the north of Panama is the Caribbean Sea, which leads to the Atlantic Ocean. Panama's Caribbean coastline is 800 miles (1,290 km) long. The Pacific Ocean is to the south. This coastline measures 1,060 miles (1,700 km). The nation of Costa Rica lies to the west, and Colombia is to the east.

Nicaragua

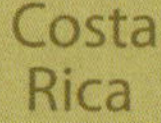

Barú

Coiba Island

Map Legend

Capital City

SCALE

350 Miles

350 Kilometers

Barú

Barú is an inactive volcano near the border of Costa Rica. At 11,401 feet (3,475 meters), it is the highest point in Panama. Experienced climbers hike Barú.

Coiba Island

Coiba Island, located about 15 miles (24 km) off the Pacific coast, is Panama's largest island. It covers 194 square miles (500 sq. km). Coiba Island's highest point measures 1,400 feet (425 m).

Panama City

Panama City is the capital and largest city of Panama. The Spanish founded the original city in 1519. Today, Panama City, on the Pacific coast, is the country's commercial and transportation center.

Tuira River

The Tuira River is located in eastern Panama. It flows northwest to the Pacific coast. At 106 miles (170 km), this waterway is one of Panama's longest rivers.

LAND AND CLIMATE

The geography of Panama has many different features. The land includes rainforests, **cloud forests**, plains, coastal islands, and sandy beaches. Panama has lowlands and highlands.

About 40 percent of Panama's land is covered by forests.

The main geographic feature of Panama is an interior chain of mountains that stretches nearly the entire east–west length of the country. This mountain chain splits the land of Panama into a Caribbean region and Pacific region. The main ranges are the Tabasara Mountains, or Cordillera Central, in the west and the Cordillera de San Blas in the east. An area of lowland separates the two *cordilleras*, which is Spanish for "mountain ranges."

In eastern Panama is the Darién region, also called the Darién Gap. This remote area of jungle runs from Panama City to Colombia. It covers about 12 million acres (4.9 million hectares). The region, accessible only by boat, has few visitors. Some Indigenous Peoples live there.

Hundreds of islands lie near Panama's northern coastline. Bocas del Toro and San Blas are two archipelagoes, or large groups of islands. The Pearl Islands are located off the southern coast of Panama. The largest of those islands is called Del Rey.

Many rivers flow over Panama's land. Most are small, emptying into the Caribbean Sea or Pacific Ocean. The Sixaola, Indio, La Miel, and Chagres Rivers drain into the Caribbean. The Chepo and Chucunaque Rivers, as well as the Tuira, flow into the Pacific. Panama has no natural lakes. Lakes such as Gatún and Alajuela, or Madden, are artificial. This means they were created by people.

The typical climate of Panama is tropical, with warm temperatures, moist air, and clouds. The coldest weather is found at the highest elevations. Coastal temperatures in Panama rarely go below about 80 degrees Fahrenheit (27 degrees Celsius).

In the Pacific coast region, there are wet and dry seasons. During the dry season, which usually begins in mid-December, northeasterly winds blow across the landscape. May marks the beginning of the wet season. Temperatures cool slightly, winds decrease, and humidity increases. Panama's Caribbean coast region is typically rainy. The average rainfall can be double that of the Pacific coast.

Land and Climate BY THE NUMBERS

One-fourth
Portion of Panama's land that is treeless plains.

About 1,000
Number of Panama's Pacific islands.

128 Inches
Average annual rainfall along the Caribbean coast. (325 centimeters)

More Than 500
Number of rivers in Panama.

Zapatilla Key is part of the Bocas del Toro archipelago. The term *key* comes from the Spanish word *cayo*, meaning "small island."

PLANTS AND ANIMALS

The small country of Panama is one of the most **biodiverse** regions in the world. More than 10,000 animal and plant **species** thrive in its diverse habitats. Panama's location at the junction of North America and South America has also contributed to many animal species moving from one continent to another over time.

Capuchin monkeys, marmosets, and Geoffroy's tamarins are examples of Panama's **primates**. Giant sea turtles lay their eggs on the beaches. Five species of big cats, including the jaguar, live in the jungles. The skies over Panama are filled with birds of all kinds. Panama is also home to slow-moving sloths and the large rodents called lesser capybaras.

Nearly 700 different types of ferns and 1,500 types of trees grow in Panama's mountains, forests, jungles, and lowlands. Among the most colorful flowers is the heliconia. Its reddish leaves resemble crab claws.

The Geoffroy's tamarin, which weighs no more than 1 pound (450 grams), is Panama's smallest monkey.

Plants and Animals BY THE NUMBERS

More Than 1,000
Number of orchid species native to Panama.

60 POUNDS
Weight of the lesser capybara. (27 kilograms)

Up to 6 Feet
Length of a jaguar, the largest type of cat in the Americas. (2 m)

NATURAL RESOURCES

Panama has various natural resources. The most abundant mineral is copper. There are smaller deposits of gold, zinc, and silver. The country also has sources of clay, limestone, and salt.

Another natural resource is Panama's forests. They are a major source of **hardwood**. Valuable mahogany and redwood are shipped around the world. This wood is used in home-building, as well as for making furniture and musical instruments. However, a recent threat to hardwood resources is deforestation. This is the cutting down of large areas of forest to obtain lumber or clear land for raising livestock. Forests are being lost at a faster rate than new tree growth can replace them.

Panama's rivers are used to produce **hydroelectricity**. More than one-half of the country's electricity is generated in this way. Coastal waters provide large quantities of shrimp. In some areas, Panama's soil is **fertile** enough to grow crops such as bananas, rice, tobacco, and sugarcane.

Natural Resources BY THE NUMBERS

353,000 Tons
Expected annual copper output from the new Cobre Panama mine when it reaches full production by 2019. (320,000 metric tons)

ABOUT 50,000 ACRES
Amount of forest Panama loses each year. (20,000 hectares)

30% Portion of land in Panama that is used for farming.

Some of Panama's farmland supports plantations, or large farms, where coffee beans are grown.

TOURISM

Millions of tourists visit Panama every year. Many of them appreciate the country's historic cities and beautiful beaches. Others explore Panama's rainforests. A number of visitors want to see the huge ships that pass through the Panama Canal. The Miraflores Visitor Center has exhibits and the best views.

Tourists can travel about 5 miles (8 km) from Casco Viejo to see the ruins of Panama City's first cathedral.

Panama City is a popular stop for travelers to Central America. They find historic churches and universities, green parks, and live-music clubs. Casco Viejo, Spanish for "old town," is the city's historic district. This area was built in 1674. The Museum of Biodiversity, or Biomuseo, opened in 2014. It is located by the Pacific entrance to the Panama Canal. Exhibits highlight the natural world's diversity and the importance of the isthmus of Panama.

The colorful modern Biomuseo building was designed by celebrated architect Frank Gehry.

A popular destination, about two hours by car or bus west of Panama City, is Anton's Valley, or El Valle de Antón. Here, a village sits in the crater, or bowl-shaped top, of an inactive volcano. Visitors can enjoy hiking, horseback riding, and bird-watching in a mountainous area that offers spectacular views.

Panama's ecotourism activities have grown in recent years. This form of tourism allows people to visit natural areas, observe the animal and plant life, and learn about the environment without damaging it. Panama's ecotourist sites include cloud forests, mountains, coastlines, and rainforests.

Many ecotourists visit Darién National Park in eastern Panama. It is the nation's largest protected region. The park spans 1.5 million acres (600,000 hectares). Sandy beaches, rocky coastlines, swamps with **mangroves**, and a wide variety of animal and plant species can all be seen in the park. Scientists have also found **artifacts** here from the area's early peoples.

Just off the Caribbean coast of Panama are the 365 San Blas Islands. Tourists visit this remote area for its natural beauty and Indigenous culture. Surfers are more likely to visit the Bocas del Toro Islands, where the waves are some of the world's best.

Tourism BY THE NUMBERS

1760 Year Panama City's cathedral was built.

$4.3 Billion Amount of money spent by visitors to Panama in 2016.

43,000 Square Feet Total square footage of Biomuseo. (4,000 sq. m)

16 Number of national parks in Panama.

Some visitors to the San Blas Islands enjoy snorkeling in the clear coastal waters.

INDUSTRY

In the 21st century, Panama has had one of the world's fastest-growing economies. Between 2001 and 2013, the annual growth rate of the country's **gross domestic product** (GDP) was more than 7 percent. In 2016, the GDP of Panama totaled about $93 billion. That was an increase of 5 percent from the previous year.

The country has a large construction industry. Thousands of new jobs in this industry were created by a major expansion of the Panama Canal from 2007 to 2016. This project allowed larger ships to use the canal. Tolls paid by ships crossing the canal are an important source of income for Panama.

Many factories in Panama produce cement and other materials for the construction industry. Some factories process the country's agricultural products. For example, mills produce sugar from sugarcane.

Industry BY THE NUMBERS

1.6 Million Total number of workers in Panama.

About 20 % Portion of the country's GDP related to the Panama Canal.

Almost 1/5 Fraction of the country's workers with jobs in manufacturing, construction, or other industries that create products.

More than 13,500 vessels pass through the Panama Canal each year.

GOODS AND SERVICES

Service industries make up the largest portion of Panama's economy. Workers in these industries provide services to others instead of producing goods. They work as truck drivers, bankers, teachers, doctors and nurses, hotel and restaurant staffs, and government officials. In Panama, many service jobs are related to operating the canal and providing services to shipping companies. The country also has a large banking industry.

Panama trades with many nations. However, the United States is, by far, the country's largest trading partner. Panama's **currency**, the balboa, is equal in value to the U.S. dollar, and dollars are widely used in the country to pay for goods and services.

In 2016, Panama **exported** $15 billion worth of goods. Major exports included fish, bananas, other foods, electrical machinery, and clothing. The value of the country's **imports** in 2016 totaled about $22 billion. Fuels, machinery, iron and steel, and medicines were imported. In Panama's Colón Free Trade Zone, on the Caribbean coast near the Panama Canal, raw materials are imported to make finished goods for export without being taxed.

Goods and Services BY THE NUMBERS

21% Portion of Panama's exports sold to the United States.

One-fourth Fraction of total imports purchased from the United States.

1948 Year the Colón Free Trade Zone was established.

About 65 percent of Panama's workers have service jobs.

INDIGENOUS PEOPLES

Many Indigenous Peoples lived in what is now Panama. They included the Ngabe, Kuna, Embera, and Bugle peoples. The Monagrillo lived in the area as early as 2500 BC. They produced some of the oldest pieces of pottery found in Central America.

Today, Panama's Indigenous People, sometimes called Amerindians, total nearly a half-million. That is more than 12 percent of the population of Panama. Many Indigenous Peoples live in their traditional homelands, deep in the mountains and rainforests.

The Embera travel in dugout canoes on the Chagres River. They live in houses on stilts and create detailed beadwork. Ngabe communities are located near Panama's border with Costa Rica. The Kuna people own and protect the San Blas Islands, while providing services for tourists. Kuna residents total about 50,000 there. Thousands of other Kuna people are scattered throughout the rest of the country.

Indigenous Peoples BY THE NUMBERS

LESS THAN 1%
Portion of Panamanians who are Embera.

1925 Year the Kuna people declared their independence within the nation of Panama.

More Than 1/2
Fraction of Panama's Indigenous People who are Ngabe.

The tourist industry helps support several Indigenous groups in Panama. For example, the Embera lead boat tours.

THE AGE OF EXPLORATION

During the Age of Exploration, which took place between the 15th and 17th centuries, Europeans looked for new trade routes to Asia and valuable natural resources in other parts of the world. In 1492, explorer Christopher Columbus, funded by Spain, landed in the Bahamas and other Caribbean islands. His voyages opened the Americas to European exploration.

In 1501, Rodrigo de Bastidas of Spain reached the Caribbean coast of the isthmus of Panama. He explored Panama's interior. Then, he sailed to the **West Indies**. A year later, Columbus arrived in Panama on his fourth voyage to the Americas.

Vasco Núñez de Balboa of Spain established a European settlement on the isthmus of Panama in 1510. It was named Santa María de la Antigua del Darién. In 1513, he crossed the isthmus and claimed the Pacific Ocean for Spain.

The Age of Exploration BY THE NUMBERS

About 200,000
Number of Indigenous People in Panama in 1501.

More Than 2,000
Number of Spanish settlers in Santa María de la Antigua del Darién before it was abandoned in 1524.

1519 Year Balboa was executed after he was convicted of treason charges brought by a rival Spanish leader, Pedro Arias Dávila.

Vasco Núñez de Balboa was the first European known to reach the Pacific Ocean.

ROAD TO INDEPENDENCE

Throughout the 17th century, Spain valued Panama as part of its trading route. Gold and silver from South America were brought by ship to Panama's Pacific coast. Then, mules transported these metals north over the isthmus for shipment across the Atlantic to Spain. At that time, thousands of Europeans, as well as Africans brought to Panama to work as slaves, lived on the isthmus.

Military leader Simón Bolívar led the fighting in New Granada for freedom from Spain.

By the mid-1700s, Panama's value to Spain had decreased. Raids by English pirates had damaged Panamanian ports, and many Spanish ships were captured. In 1739, Spain made Panama part of the colony of New Granada, which included Colombia. When Colombia won its independence from Spain in 1821, Panama joined it.

In the 1880s and 1890s, a French company tried and failed to build a canal across the isthmus. Thousands of workers died from disease. Early in the next century, the United States succeeded in completing a canal.

Investors in the French project to dig a canal in Panama lost more than $250 million.

U.S. president Theodore Roosevelt wanted to shorten the travel time by ship from the eastern United States to Asia. However, the government of Colombia refused to allow a U.S.-built canal. In 1903, the United States helped Panamanian rebels win independence from Colombia. The new Panamanian government then agreed to a treaty permitting the United States to build and operate the canal. Under the treaty, the United States also controlled a strip of land, the Panama Canal Zone, on both sides of the waterway.

By the second half of the 20th century, U.S. control of the canal had become unpopular in Panama. A new treaty went into effect in 1978. Under this treaty, the United States agreed to gradually transfer control of the canal and the surrounding Canal Zone to Panama. The transfer was completed in 1999.

While the transfer was in process, the United States sent troops to Panama in 1989. They were sent to capture General Manuel Noriega, who was ruling the country as a **dictator**. Noriega surrendered in 1990. He was in prison in Panama when he died in 2017.

Road to Independence BY THE NUMBERS

1671 Year adventurer Henry Morgan, supported by the English government, attacked and destroyed the original Panama City.

Almost $375 Million
Cost to build the Panama Canal in the early 1900s, which equals about $8.6 billion today.

More Than 27,000
Number of U.S. troops who invaded Panama in 1989 to remove General Noriega from power.

In Panama, many citizens who opposed Manuel Noriega celebrated the U.S. invasion of their country in 1989.

POPULATION

More than 3.7 million people live in Panama. Most of the population is located in the center of the country, around the Panama Canal. However, there is also a large population in and around the western city of David, on the Pacific coast.

About two-thirds of Panamanians live in **urban** areas. Panama City and the communities around it have a population of more than 1.7 million. David and Colón are the country's next-largest cities.

The rate of population growth is gradually decreasing in Panama. One-fourth of the country's people are under 15 years old, but more than half the population is age 25 or older. Women in Panama have two children, on average. This is a lower figure than in almost one-half of the world's countries.

Poverty is a problem for many Panamanians. Nationwide, almost one-fourth of people live in poverty. This problem is most widespread outside urban areas.

Population BY THE NUMBERS

131 People Per Square Mile
Population density of Panama. (50 per sq. km)

63% Portion of the country's urban population that lives in Panama City.

78.8 Years
Average **life expectancy** in Panama, a higher figure than in more than two-thirds of the world's countries.

About 200,000 people live in the north-central port city of Colón.

POLITICS AND GOVERNMENT

As in the United States, Panama's national government has executive, legislative, and judicial branches. Panama's current **constitution**, which describes the powers of each branch and how officials are chosen, went into effect in 1972. Panama is a republic. This means the head of state, or highest-level government official, is elected.

Panama's head of state is the president. He or she serves a five-year term and can be elected only once. A vice president is also elected to serve for one five-year term.

Panama's legislature, the National Assembly, has one house. Assembly members are elected for five-year terms and can seek reelection. The National Assembly passes the country's laws. It also approves the government's budget and treaties with other nations. The Supreme Court is Panama's highest-level court. It can decide whether laws violate the constitution.

Politics and Government BY THE NUMBERS

71 Number of members in the National Assembly.

5 Number of political parties in Panama.

18 YEARS OLD Age at which people in Panama are eligible to vote.

Panama's president delivers an annual State of the Nation speech to the National Assembly to report on new government policies.

CULTURAL GROUPS

Spanish is the official language of Panama.

Until the 1900s, most Panamanians could trace their **ancestors** to the area's Indigenous Peoples, Spanish colonists, or Africans brought to Panama as slaves. Then, canal workers from around the world, and especially the West Indies, also contributed to the country's diversity. Today, most Panamanians are mestizo. They have mixed Amerindian and European origins. Almost one-tenth of Panamanians are people of black or African descent. People with mixed African and European ancestry and Panamanians with European origins only each make up about 7 percent of the population.

Almost everyone in Panama speaks Spanish, but many Indigenous Peoples also continue to use their native languages. Indigenous languages include Ngabere, Buglere, Kuna, and Embera. Some Panamanians also speak English Creole. This language is influenced by English and languages of West Africa.

Some Indigenous children are able to use their native languages at community schools.

The large majority of Panamanians follow the Roman Catholic religion. There are also sizable Jewish and Protestant populations. Some Indigenous Panamanians practice traditional beliefs. Others follow a mix of traditional religion and Catholicism.

Panama's Indigenous Peoples each have their own cultures. The Kuna are known for a colorful **textile** art called *molas*. Ngabe men dress traditionally in homemade bellbottom pants, straw hats, and rubber boots. Traditional dress for women includes decorative bright-colored dresses. Males and females decorate their bodies with tattoos.

For people of all cultural groups, opportunities for education expanded in the second half of the 20th century. Children between the ages of four and fourteen are required to attend school. Today, almost everyone in the country can read and write. The nation has several institutions of higher learning, including the University of Panama in Panama City.

Cultural Groups BY THE NUMBERS

65% Portion of people in Panama who are mestizo.

1935 Year the University of Panama was founded.

85% Portion of the population that follows the Roman Catholic faith.

Molas are part of traditional Kuna clothing. However, the Kuna sell their handmade *molas* to tourists as artworks.

ARTS AND ENTERTAINMENT

The performing and visual arts of Panama are rooted in the nation's diversity. Hispanic influences mix with Amerindian, African, and U.S. cultures. Today, the people of Panama appreciate and continue to contribute to this vibrant cultural mix.

Panama's first musical traditions were created by the region's Indigenous Peoples. The *gammu burwi* is a bamboo **panpipe** that the Kuna play. Other Indigenous instruments include a three-string violin called the *rabel* and the *mejorana*, which resembles a ukulele.

The *mejorana*, a five-string folk guitar, is typically carved from a block of wood.

Rubén Blades, who also works as a television and film actor, performs with his band around the world.

The music probably most closely associated with Panama is salsa. This popular dance music blends Cuban rhythms with elements of jazz and rock music. Salsa is typically performed at 150 beats per minute. Rubén Blades, born in Panama City, is one of the world's most successful salsa musicians. He has received eight Grammy Awards for his work. In 2017, Panamanian songwriter Erika Ender won a Latin Grammy Award for her hit song "Despacito."

The country's largest festival is **Carnival**. Lively parades are held in the streets. Artists play folk songs, salsa, and reggae, a style of music that originated in Jamaica. Panamanian musicians Kafu Banton and Apache Ness perform reggae.

Jazz music, with its American roots in work songs and spirituals, became popular in Panama in the early 1900s. Violeta Green of Colón was one of the country's first jazz vocalists, or singers. Panamanian pianist Danilo Pérez founded the country's first jazz festival in 2003.

Theater is also an important part of the arts in Panama. The National Theater, or El Teatro Nacional, in Panama City's Casco Viejo district celebrated its 100th anniversary in 2008. Theatergoers have been treated to Italian opera, classical symphonies, and ballet performances.

Panama's artists express themselves in various art forms. Juan Manuel Cedeno, who lived from 1915 to 1997, was a portrait painter and **muralist**. Brooke Alfaro works as a painter and a video artist. His art examines the everyday lives of Panamanians in humorous and bold ways. Sculptor Isabel de Obalida creates her sculptures out of glass. Her father is painter Guillermo Trujillo, who pays respect to Panama and its Indigenous Peoples in his work.

Arts and Entertainment BY THE NUMBERS

MORE THAN 25 MILLION Number of copies that *Siembra*, a salsa album by Rubén Blades, has sold.

17 Years Old Age at which Violeta Green began performing.

16 Weeks Number of weeks that Erika Ender's "Despacito" was number one on the *Billboard* Hot 100.

The National Theater in Panama City features several balconies and a ceiling mural by Roberto Lewis, a Panamanian painter born in 1874.

SPORTS

People in Panama watch and participate in a variety of sports, such as basketball, cycling, and tennis. However, the country's national sport is baseball. Rod Carew, born in Gatún in 1945, was the first athlete from Panama elected to the Baseball Hall of Fame, honoring the best players in Major League Baseball. Carew played for the Minnesota Twins and California Angels. He is one of the few players to have more than 3,000 hits in his Major League career.

Panamanian track and field champion Andrea Ferris earned gold medals at six Central American Championships from 2007 to 2015.

Mariano Rivera grew up in Panama City, where he played baseball with his friends. The children bent milk cartons to form mitts because they could not afford baseball gloves. Rivera began pitching for the New York Yankees in 1995. By the end of his long career in 2013, he had become one of the best **relief pitchers** of all time.

Irving Saladino, from Colón, had the skills to become a professional baseball player. Instead, he continued to train in track and field. He won the long jump at the 2002 Central American Championships. In 2008, at the Summer Games in Beijing, China, Saladino became the first athlete from Panama to win an Olympic gold medal.

Mariano Rivera helped the Yankees win five World Series titles.

Soccer is played in every region of Panama. In 2017, the national men's team qualified for the World Cup, the highest-level international tournament, for the first time ever. Panama teammates Ismael Diaz, Fidel Escobar, and Michael Murillo also play for professional teams in other countries.

Cricket is another popular sport in Panama. Similar to baseball, cricket is played with a bat and ball. West Indian cricket players who came to the area to help build the Panama Canal brought the game with them. They played on Sunday, their only day off, with local residents.

Panamanian boxer Roberto Durán won world titles in four different weight classes during his career. Durán, born in Panama City in 1951, grew up in poverty. As a young boy, he worked shining shoes and selling newspapers. He learned to box at age 16 and won his first championship in 1972. Durán is often called one of the greatest fighters of all time.

Sports BY THE NUMBERS

1928 Year Panama participated in its first Summer Olympic Games, in Amsterdam, the Netherlands.

.328 Career batting average of Rod Carew.

16 Number of years Mariano Rivera played in the postseason with the New York Yankees.

Roberto Durán beat American boxer Sugar Ray Leonard in a June 1980 championship fight.

Mapping Panama

We use many tools to interpret maps and to understand the locations of features such as cities, states, lakes, and rivers. The map below has many tools to help interpret information on the map of Panama.

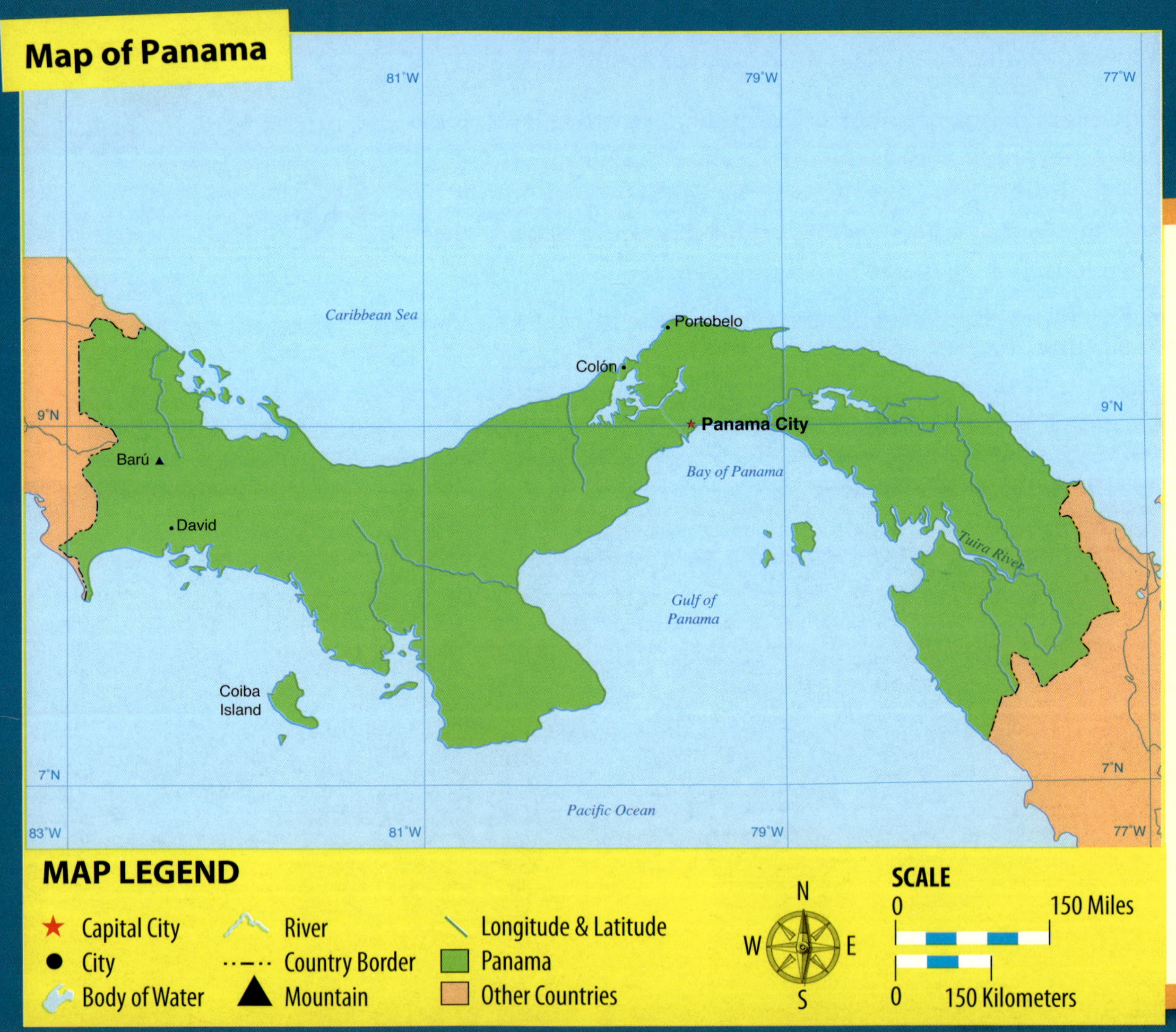

Mapping Tools

- The compass rose shows north, south, east, and west. The points in-between represent northeast, northwest, southeast, and southwest.
- The map scale shows that the distances on a map represent much longer distances in real life. If you measure the distance between objects on a map, you can use the map scale to calculate the actual distance in miles or kilometers between those two points.
- The lines of latitude and longitude are long lines that appear on maps. The lines of latitude run east to west and measure how far north or south of the equator a place is located. The lines of longitude run north to south and measure how far east or west of the Prime Meridian a place is located. A location on a map can be found by using the two numbers where latitude and longitude meet. This number is called a coordinate and is written using degrees and direction. For example, Panama City would be found at 9°N and 79.5°W on a map.

Map It!

Using the map and the appropriate tools, complete the activities below.

Locating with latitude and longitude

1. Which city is found at 9.3°N and 80°W?
2. What is located at 8.8°N and 82.5°W?
3. Which city is found on the map using the coordinates 8.4°N and 82.4°W?

Distances between points

4. Using the map scale and a ruler, calculate the approximate distance between the cities of Panama City and David.
5. Using the map scale and a ruler, calculate the approximate distance between Panama City and Portobelo.
6. Using the map scale and a ruler, calculate the approximate distance between Portobelo and Colón.

ANSWERS 1. Colón 2. Barú 3. David 4. 200 miles (320 km) 5. 42 miles (68 km) 6. 24 miles (39 km)

Quiz Time

Test your knowledge of Panama by answering these questions.

1 What is the capital of Panama?

2 In what year was the Panama Canal completed?

3 What is the highest point in the country?

4 How many islands are part of Panama?

5 What is Panama's largest protected region?

6 What is the name of Panama City's historic district?

7 How many Indigenous People, sometimes called Amerindians, live in Panama today?

8 In which year did Rodrigo de Bastidas reach the Caribbean coast of the isthmus of Panama?

9 What percentage of Panama's population follows the Roman Catholic faith?

10 Who was the first athlete from Panama to win an Olympic gold medal?

ANSWERS

1. Panama City
2. 1914
3. Barú
4. More than 1,600
5. Darién National Park
6. Casco Viejo
7. Nearly a half-million
8. 1501
9. 85 percent
10. Irving Saladino

Key Words

ancestors: members of one's cultural group or family who lived in the past
artifacts: objects made or changed by people in the past
biodiverse: related to the number and variety of living things in a region
Carnival: a festival, usually in February or early March, celebrated before the Roman Catholic religious period of Lent
Central America: a region of North America that extends from the southern border of Mexico to the northern border of South America
cloud forests: high-elevation tropical forests that receive moisture from contact with clouds instead of from rainfall
colony: a country or area controlled by another country
constitution: a written document stating a country's basic principles and laws
currency: the form of money that a country uses
dictator: a ruler who has absolute power and allows people very little freedom
economy: the wealth and resources of a country or area
exported: sold to other countries
fertile: referring to land that is suitable for growing crops or other plants
gross domestic product: the total value of goods produced and services provided in a country during a year
hardwood: the wood, usually very hard, from a type of tree that has broad leaves rather than needles
hydroelectricity: electricity produced using the energy of moving water, such as in a river
imports: goods that a country buys from other countries
life expectancy: the number of years a person is expected to live
mangroves: trees or shrubs that grow in swamps with salty water and that have roots partly above the ground
muralist: an artist who creates wall paintings
panpipe: a wind instrument consisting of pipes of different lengths tied together in a row
primates: animal species that include humans, monkeys, and apes
relief pitchers: pitchers who specialize in replacing another pitcher during a baseball game
species: groups of individuals with common characteristics
textile: woven or knit fabric and the thread or yard used to make it
urban: relating to a city or town
West Indies: a chain of islands separating the Caribbean Sea from the Atlantic Ocean

Index

Log on to www.av2books.com

AV² by Weigl brings you media enhanced books that support active learning. Go to www.av2books.com, and enter the special code found on page 2 of this book. You will gain access to enriched and enhanced content that supplements and complements this book. Content includes video, audio, weblinks, quizzes, a slide show, and activities.

AV² Online Navigation

Book Pages
AV² pages directly correspond to pages in the book.

Audio
Listen to sections of the book read aloud.

Video
Watch informative video clips.

Embedded Weblinks
Gain additional information for research.

Key Words
Study vocabulary, and complete a matching word activity.

Try This!
Complete activities and hands-on experiments.

Quizzes
Test your knowledge.

Slide Show
View images and captions, and prepare a presentation.

AV² was built to bridge the gap between print and digital. We encourage you to tell us what you like and what you want to see in the future.

Sign up to be an AV² Ambassador at www.av2books.com/ambassador.

Due to the dynamic nature of the Internet, some of the URLs and activities provided as part of AV² by Weigl may have changed or ceased to exist. AV² by Weigl accepts no responsibility for any such changes. All media enhanced books are regularly monitored to update addresses and sites in a timely manner. Contact AV² by Weigl at 1-866-649-3445 or av2books@weigl.com with any questions, comments, or feedback.